Dear Parents,

This is a Stepping Stone Book™ by the Berenstains. We have drawn on decades of experience creating books for children to make these books not only easy to read but also exciting, suspenseful, and meaningful enough to be read over and over again. Our chapter books will include mysteries, life lessons, action and adventure tales, and laugh-out-loud stories. They are written in short sentences and simple language that will take your youngsters happily past beginning readers and into the exciting world of chapter books they can read all by themselves!

Happy reading!

The Berenstains

BOOKS IN THIS SERIES:

The Goofy, Goony Guy

The Haunted Lighthouse

The Runamuck Dog Show

The Wrong Crowd

Copyright © 2001 by Berenstain Enterprises, Inc. All rights reserved under
International and Pan-American Copyright Conventions. Published in the
United States by Random House, Inc., New York, and simultaneously in Canada
by Random House of Canada Limited, Toronto.

www.randomhouse.com/kids
www.berenstainbears.com

Library of Congress Cataloging-in-Publication Data
Berenstain, Stan, 1923–
The goofy, goony guy / by Stan & Jan Berenstain.
    p. cm.
(A stepping stone book)
SUMMARY: The new cub in Sister Bear's second-grade class looks and acts so
strange that Sister avoids him when he tries to make friends.
ISBN 0-375-81270-9 (trade) — ISBN 0-375-91270-3 (lib. bdg.)
[1. Individuality—Fiction. 2. Friendship—Fiction. 3. Schools—Fiction.
4. Bears—Fiction.] I. Berenstain, Jan, 1923– . II. Title.
PZ7.B4483 Go 2001 [Fic]—dc21 00-062549

Printed in the United States of America July 2001
10 9 8 7 6 5 4 3 2 1

RANDOM HOUSE and colophon are registered trademarks and
A STEPPING STONE BOOK and colophon are trademarks of Random House, Inc.

The Goofy, Goony Guy

The Berenstains

A STEPPING STONE BOOK™

Random House 🏠 New York

Sister Bear was in second grade. Teacher Jane was her teacher. There wasn't much new in second grade.

But today there was.

There was a new cub in class.

Sister saw him when she came into the room. He was standing at the front with Teacher Jane.

He was a goofy, goony-looking guy.

His ears stuck out.

His teeth stuck out.

His fur stuck out.

In fact, everything on him seemed to stick out.

Teacher Jane wrote on the board.

She wrote the goofy, goony guy's name.

His name was Herbert Harold Armfoot.

Herbert Harold Armfoot?

"The Third," said the goofy, goony guy.

"I beg your pardon?" said Teacher Jane.

"I am Herbert Harold Armfoot the Third," he said. "My grandfather was the first. My father was the second, and I am the third."

"I see," said Teacher Jane.

She wrote "III" after the new cub's name.

"That's the Roman three," she said. "We haven't had those yet. But that's how you write 'the Third' after somebody's name."

That was okay with Sister.

"Herbert, say hello to your new class."

The new cub said, "Hi" and gave a little wave. He sure *was* a goofy, goony guy. He even waved funny.

"Now, Herbert," said Teacher Jane, "we'll find a seat for you."

She looked out over the class.

There were three empty seats.

There was one in the back row.

There was one near the door.

There was one in the row next

to Sister, one seat up from her.

"Hmm," said Teacher Jane as she looked around the room.

Please, thought Sister, *please don't put the goofy, goony guy near me.*

"Sister, would you please raise your hand?" said Teacher Jane.

Sister raised her hand. She didn't raise it high. But she raised it.

"Herbert," said Teacher Jane, "you go sit in the empty seat near Sister."

Sister brought her hand down real quick. But not quick enough.

The goofy, goony guy saw her. He gave her a big grin. He sat in the empty seat. Then he turned and grinned at Sister again.

Lizzy Bruin was Sister's best friend. She sat behind Sister. Lizzy leaned forward.

"You know something?" said Lizzy. "I think he likes you."

Sister's heart sank.

Please, she thought. *Please don't let the goofy, goony guy like me!*

Teacher Jane was writing on the board again. It was time for math.

The class had learned to add.

They had learned to take away.

They had learned to multiply.

"We have already learned to

add, take away, and multiply," said Teacher Jane. "Today we will learn to divide."

She had put two things on the board. One looked like this:

$$30 \div 10 =$$

The other looked like this:

$$10 \overline{)30}$$

"Those are both about dividing," she said. "They look different, but they mean the same thing. They both ask the same question. How many tens are there in thirty? Does anybody wish to tell us?"

Hands went up.

Teacher Jane called on William. "Yes, William?"

"There are three tens in thirty," said William.

"How do we know that?" asked Teacher Jane.

"Because three *times* ten is thirty. That means there are three tens *in* thirty."

"Thank you, William," said Teacher Jane. "This kind of dividing is called 'short division.'"

That was okay with Sister.

"There's another kind of dividing called 'long division,'" said Teacher Jane. "We shall learn about long division later in the year."

That was okay with Sister, too. In fact, school was okay with Sister.

She liked spelling.

She liked science—especially when it was about nature.

Sister even liked math. So much so that she almost forgot about the new cub.

But not quite.

Teacher Jane wrote more examples on the board.

Cubs raised their hands and gave answers.

But not Sister.

She was too busy trying not to think about the goofy, goony guy.

At playtime, Sister and her friends took turns turning for double Dutch. This week it was Sister and Lizzy's turn.

They got the double Dutch rope from Teacher Bob. He was yard teacher.

There were two long ropes. You needed two ropes for double Dutch.

Sister held one end of each rope. Lizzy took hold of the other ends. The jumpers were lined up.

Nellie was first in line. Sister and Lizzy started turning. Soon the ropes were turning both ways.

As they turned, they chanted:

> *Double Dutch!*
> *Double Dutch!*
> *Such a much!*
> *Such a much!*
> *Rope can sting!*
> *Rope can sting!*
> *Rope can sting*
> *Like anything!*

The ropes were turning fast. Nellie rocked back and forth.

Then she jumped into the turning ropes. She took her turn.

Next came Jill.

Next came Amy.

Next came Emma.

Emma wasn't so lucky.

The ropes stung her legs. She got all tangled. They had to start over.

Double Dutch!
Double Dutch!
Such a much!
Such a much!
Rope can sting!
Rope can sting!
Rope can sting
Like anything!

The ropes were turning. Jumpers were jumping.

Sister turned and chanted. She looked out over the yard. She looked over at the boys' side. There were no rules about the yard. It was just that the girls liked one side and the boys liked the other side.

The boys were playing fistball. It was like baseball. But you hit a rubber ball with your fist.

Sister looked for Brother. He was pitching. She looked for Cousin Fred. He was playing first base. Then she looked for Herbert Harold Armfoot III.

She couldn't find him. He wasn't on the boys' side.

Where was he? Then she knew.

"Hey!" cried Lizzy. "What are you doing?"

Herbert Harold Armfoot III was in the double Dutch line! And it was his turn!

He jumped into the turning ropes. He started jumping.

Sister was surprised. She stopped chanting. But she didn't stop turning. She and Lizzy turned faster. They speeded up to Red-Hot Pepper.

Whoever heard of anyone jumping double Dutch Red-Hot Pepper?

But the goofy, goony guy kept jumping.

He jumped on two feet.

He jumped on one foot.

He jumped on the other foot.

The goofy, goony guy was on fire!

The bell rang. Playtime was over.

Sister looked over at the boys' side. The fistball game had stopped.

The boys had been watching Herbert Harold Armfoot III jump.

What did the goofy, goony guy think he was doing?

He could be heading for trouble.

Sister was helping Mama in the kitchen.

They were getting ready for supper. They were at the sink. Mama was peeling and cutting apples for a pie. Sister was scraping carrots. She was standing on a high stool.

Sister was quiet. The room was quiet. The whole house was quiet. Brother was up in his room. Papa was out in his shop.

Scrape, scrape, scrape went the carrot scraper.

Mama looked at Sister. She was staring out the window.

"A penny for your thoughts," said Mama.

"Huh?" said Sister.

"You seem deep in thought," said Mama.

"There's a new cub in class," said Sister.

"Oh," said Mama.

"Teacher Jane sat him near me," said Sister.

"I see," said Mama.

"He keeps looking at me," said Sister.

"Perhaps he wants to make friends," said Mama.

"Yeah, but you ought to see him," said Sister. "He's a goofy, goony guy. His ears stick out. His teeth stick out. His fur sticks out. Everything on him sticks out. He's the goofiest, gooniest-looking guy you *ever* saw."

"Well, now," said Mama. "It's not what we look like that counts. It's what's inside that counts."

"You mean like lungs, livers, and gizzards?" said Sister.

"You know perfectly well I don't mean lungs, livers, and gizzards," said Mama. "It's the kind of person we are that counts. What kind of person is the new cub?"

"I told you," said Sister. "He's a goofy, goony person. Even his name is funny."

"What's his name?" asked Mama.

"Herbert Harold Armfoot the Third," said Sister.

Mama tried to stop herself from laughing.

But she couldn't.

It came out a snort.

"See?" said Sister. "Even *you* laughed."

"I wasn't laughing at that," said Mama. "I just remembered something funny that someone said to me."

"Uh-huh," said Sister. "You ought to see what he did at play-time!"

"What?" said Mama.

"He came over to the girls' side and jumped double Dutch!" said Sister.

"What's wrong with that?" asked Mama.

"What's wrong with that?" said Sister. "It just isn't done! That's what's wrong with it! He could get into trouble. It's a good thing the Too-Tall gang wasn't there. They'd go after him."

"Where was the Too-Tall gang?" asked Mama.

"Kicked out," said Sister. "They sassed Teacher Bob."

"I see," said Mama.

Mama cut more apples.

Sister scraped more carrots.

"Well," said Mama, "I think he was just trying to make friends. You can't have too many friends."

Sister stopped scraping. Her eyes got wide. She stared out the window. "OH NO!" she cried.

"What's wrong?" asked Mama.

"It's the goofy, goony guy! He's coming up our front steps!"

Sister dropped the scraper. She

got down from the stool.

"What are you doing?" asked Mama.

"I'm going to hide," said Sister.

The doorbell rang.

"You'll do no such thing!" said Mama.

"But, Mama," said Sister.

"Stop this," said Mama. "Go get the door. Welcome him. Bring him to me. I'd like to meet your new friend."

Sister got the door.

There he was.

As goofy and goony as ever.

"You live in a tree?" he said.

"So?" said Sister.

"So, cool," said Herbert Harold Armfoot III.

"How did you know where I lived?" asked Sister.

"I watched you get off the bus."

"I didn't see you on the bus," said Sister.

"I was there," said the goofy, goony guy. "I was in the back."

The new cub looked around.

"Hey, it's like a normal house inside," he said.

"What did you think it would be like?" asked Sister.

"I don't know. Woodpeckers?"

"Come," said Sister, "my mother wants to meet you."

They went to the kitchen.

"Mama, this is the cub I told you about."

"Welcome to our home," said Mama. "It's Herbert, isn't it? I'll tell you what. You and Sister sit down. I have some fresh-baked raisin cookies. How does that sound? And a glass of milk with honey."

"Sounds fine," said Herbert.

"Except for the honey. I can't eat honey."

A bear who can't eat honey, thought Sister. *Wouldn't you know?*

Mama set out the milk and cookies. Sister took a bite of cookie.

Herbert picked up his cookie. He started picking the raisins out.

"Er, don't you like raisins?" asked Mama.

"I always save the raisins for later," said Herbert. "They have a lot of energy. You never know when you're going to need some energy."

"Er, yes, I see," said Mama.

Sister looked at Mama.

The look said, *See what I mean!*

4

"Thank you for the milk and cook-ies," said Herbert. "Now if you don't mind, I'll have a look upstairs."

And before they knew it, he was upstairs.

Brother was in his room. He was working on a model airplane. Model airplanes were Brother's hobby. They hung from the ceiling. The walls were covered with pictures of airplanes.

Brother heard somebody say,

"Wow!" He looked around.

"This is Herbert. He's in my class," said Sister.

Herbert came into Brother's room. He looked at the pictures on the wall.

"Wow!" he said. "Captain Jimmie Bearlittle's Bee-Gee Racer— also known as the Flying Milk Bottle. And hey, Lucky Linbear's Ryan Special! And look, Wilbear and Orville Wright's first plane."

"You know your airplanes," said Brother.

"Airplanes are one of my favorite things," said Herbert.

"Sister," said Brother, "your

friend knows his airplanes."

But Sister was gone.

She had had enough airplane talk.

She had also had enough of goofy, goony guy Herbert Harold Armfoot III.

More than enough.

* * *

Sister Bear woke up the next morning. She had something on her mind. Something bad.

But she couldn't think what it was.

She stared at the ceiling.

Then she remembered. It was the goofy, goony guy.

Brother was already at breakfast when Sister came down. She was just waiting for him to say something.

He said the wrong thing.

"I like your new boyfriend," said Brother.

"HE IS *NOT* MY BOYFRIEND!"

Sister shouted. "He is not even my friend! I don't even like him!"

"Then how come he was jumping rope with you?" said Brother.

"IT WASN'T MY FAULT HE WAS JUMPING ROPE WITH ME!" shouted Sister.

Papa put down his newspaper. "Sister," he said, "that's enough shouting. And, Brother, that's quite enough teasing."

"Your papa's right," said Mama. "And that's enough talk about boyfriends. Sister's much too young for boyfriends. Now eat your breakfast. Both of you. Or you'll miss the school bus."

Sister and Lizzy always sat together on the school bus.

They sat together on the way to school. They sat together on the way home. The bus picked Lizzy up first on the way. She always saved a seat for Sister.

They were best friends. But they weren't a group.

Marcia, Gwen, and Jill were a group. They were boy-crazy. All they ever talked about was boys.

Sister climbed onto the bus. Lizzy had saved a seat.

It was the same as every morning. Except for one thing.

There was a sign.

It was taped to the seat in front.
This is what it looked like.

Sister was so mad. She couldn't believe her eyes.

"Who put that there?" she asked.

"I don't know," said Lizzy.

"What do you mean you don't know? You were sitting here," said Sister.

"I was looking out the window," said Lizzy. "I don't know who put it there. And that's the truth."

Sister was furious. She tore off the sign. She crumpled it up.

She looked around the bus. There was the goofy, goony guy sitting in the back.

He gave Sister a little wave.

"He did it, didn't he?" said Sister.

"Maybe," said Lizzy. "But I didn't see him."

Sister didn't say another word. She just sat there and steamed.

She was still steaming when the bus pulled to a stop. She tried to get off the bus.

There was pushing and shoving.

There was a jam at the front of the bus.

There was giggling.

Sister got off the bus. Then she saw why there was giggling.

It was another sign. This one was on the sidewalk in chalk. It said:

HERBERT IS MAD ABOUT SISTER
X X X X X X X X X

But not nearly as mad as Sister was. She tried to rub it out with her foot.

But all she did was smear it.

"That Herbert," said Sister. "I'm going to—"

"But he couldn't have done it," said Lizzy. "He was on the bus. Look, he's just getting off."

But Sister wasn't so sure.

She turned and looked at Herbert.

If looks could kill, Herbert would have been dead.

But Herbert just gave Sister another little wave.

The bell rang.

"Come on," said Lizzy. "We have to get in line."

"I know how he wrote that sign," said Sister. "He did it yesterday before he came over."

"Came over where?" asked Lizzy.

"To my house!" said Sister.

"He came over to your house?" said Lizzy. "Boy, he's got it bad."

"That's right," said Sister. "I was looking out the window. There he was, big as life and *twice* as goony."

Teacher Jane was standing at the door of her room. She greeted each cub.

"Good morning, Marvin," she said.

"Good morning, Teacher Jane," said Marvin.

"Good morning, Lizzy," said Teacher Jane.

"Good morning, Teacher Jane," said Lizzy.

"Good morning, Sister," said Teacher Jane.

"Good morning, Teacher Jane," said Sister.

But she said it through her teeth. She was still steamed.

And when she saw the blackboard, smoke came out of her ears.

The biggest sign yet was on the blackboard.

It said:

Sister was mad! She couldn't find her seat. When she found it, she sat down hard. She stared ahead.

That goon, that goof, that creep, she thought.

Teacher Jane saw the board. She wasn't happy.

"Erasing helpers, please," she said.

Arnold and Maxine were erasing helpers that week.

They erased the board.

But they couldn't erase Sister's anger.

5

Sister was mad all day. She had a hard time concentrating.

She messed up a spelling test.

She messed up a math quiz.

She even messed up turning double Dutch at playtime.

But that wasn't the worst thing. The worst thing was how Marcia, Gwen, and Jill kept giggling.

Sister looked across the yard at the boys' side. She looked for Herbert. He wasn't playing fistball.

She saw him in a far corner of the yard. What was he doing? He was looking at a tree. He was looking at a tree?

That's all the Too-Tall gang has to see, thought Sister. A new cub looking at a tree or a flower—or jumping double Dutch.

Poor Herbert. The Too-Tall gang would go after him.

But so what?

Sister couldn't have cared less.

After school, Sister went straight up to her room. She closed the door and sat at her desk.

She could still see those dumb love notes.

She could still hear Marcia, Gwen, and Jill giggling.

Her notebook was on her desk. She wrote in it only when there was something on her mind.

She opened it and began to write. She wrote and wrote and wrote.

This is what she wrote:

I HATE HERBERT HAROLD ARMFOOT III
I HATE HERBERT HAROLD ARMFOOT III
I HATE HERBERT HAROLD ARMFOOT III
I HATE HERBERT HAROLD ARMFOOT III
I HATE HERBERT HAROLD ARMFOOT III
I HATE HERBERT HAROLD ARMFOOT III
I HATE HERBERT HAROLD ARMFOOT III
I HATE HERBERT HAROLD ARMFOOT III
I HATE HERBERT HAROLD ARMFOOT III
I HATE HERBERT HAROLD ARMFOOT III
I HATE HERBERT HAROLD ARMFOOT III
BT HAROLD ARMFOOT II

She looked at what she had written.

Herbert *was* a goofy, goony guy. But she really didn't hate him that much. What she really hated was all that giggling.

She crossed out the whole page with a big X.

Then she heard knocking.

It wasn't at the door.

It was at the window.

It was Herbert. He was thirty feet off the ground. He was knocking at her window! What did he think he was doing? He could fall and break his whole goofy, goony body.

She went to the window. She let him in.

"WHAT DO YOU WANT?" she shouted.

He climbed in.

"There's something I had to tell you. I didn't do it," he said. "I didn't put the sign on the bus. I didn't write on the sidewalk. I didn't write on the blackboard."

"Who did?" asked Sister. But then she remembered giggling.

Now she knew!

She thought of her notebook. She had left it open. She rushed over and shut it.

"Okay. I'll take your word for it," said Sister. "But you can't climb into people's windows."

"I had to tell you I didn't do it," said Herbert. "Besides, I climb trees all the time. It's one of my favorite things."

"How could you tell this was my room?" asked Sister.

"You've got paper flowers stuck to your window," said Herbert. "I have a question for you: What's this book you shut?"

He opened it. Sister got angry all over again.

"That's my notebook," said

Sister. "Don't you dare look at it!"

She shut it again. But his fingers were still in it.

"Ouch!" he said.

"And that's not all. I don't want a boyfriend. But if I did, it wouldn't be you!"

"But—" said Herbert.

"So march yourself down the stairs!"

"But—" said Herbert.

"And out the door!"

Herbert went slowly down the stairs.

Sister watched to be sure he left.

But he didn't leave.

Papa's main hobby was fly-fishing. He used fake flies for bait. He made them himself.

He was working on one when Herbert passed his study.

"Hello," said Papa. "You must be the new cub."

"That's right," said Sister. She had followed Herbert down the stairs. "His name is Herbert Harold Armfoot."

"The Third," said Herbert.

"I beg your pardon," said Papa.

"I'm Herbert Harold Armfoot the Third," he said. "My grandfather was the first. My father was the second. And I'm the third."

"I see," said Papa.

Papa was making a fly out of feathers and fine silk thread. It was very hard work. Sometimes he had to use a glass lens.

"That's a very nice fly, sir," said Herbert. "Can I make a suggestion?"

"Sure," said Papa. "Do you like fly-fishing?"

"It's one of my favorite things," said Herbert. "Try tying some silk around the base of the wings. When you reel it in, they'll flutter."

"Like a live fly!" said Papa.

"Exactly," said Herbert Harold Armfoot III.

"Do you have any other ideas?" said Papa.

"Well," said Herbert, "I've had good success using dragonflies for bass."

"Really?" said Papa. "What do you use for eyes?"

"Those little red glass beads make great eyes," said Herbert. "You

know, the kind that come in bead kits. I'm sure Sister has some."

"Indeed," said Papa. "Did you hear that, Sister? . . . Sister?"

But Sister was gone.

She had had enough talk about fly-fishing.

She had had more than enough of Herbert Harold Armfoot III.

She stomped upstairs to her room and slammed the door. She sat at her desk and opened her notebook and wrote.

One guess what she wrote.

I HATE HERBERT HAROLD ARMFOOT III
I HATE HERBERT HAROLD ARMFOOT III
I HATE HERBERT HAROLD ARMFOOT III
I HATE HERBERT HAROLD ARMFOOT III
I HATE HERBERT HAROLD ARMFOOT III
I HATE HERBERT ...

The Too-Tall gang was back at school. And they were back to doing what they liked. They liked to pick on younger cubs. New cubs were best.

It didn't take them long to find Herbert.

"What did you say your name was?" said Too-Tall.

"I didn't say," said Herbert.

Brother came over. He stuck up for Herbert.

"His name is Herbert Harold Armfoot," said Brother.

"The Third," said Herbert.

"What's that supposed to mean?" said Skuzz. He was Too-Tall's right-hand cub.

Herbert told about his grand-father and father and why he was called "the Third."

"Well," said Too-Tall, "I got news for you. If you don't look out, you're gonna be Herbert Harold Armfoot the Last."

The gang walked away, laugh-ing.

"Look," said Brother. "They're pretty mean. If they come after you, give me a yell. Or go tell the yard teacher."

"I'll be okay," said Herbert. "I can take care of myself."

Four big fourth graders against one second grader? thought Brother. He didn't think so.

It didn't take long.

The Too-Tall gang came after Herbert the next day. It was at play-time.

Some second graders were playing dodgeball. It was Herbert's turn to go in the middle.

The Too-Tall gang took over the game.

They threw the ball as hard as

they could. But they couldn't hit Herbert.

He was too quick.

He jumped.

He twisted.

He turned.

He dodged.

"Hey!" shouted Too-Tall. "You keep dodging!"

"That's why it's called *dodge-ball*," said Herbert. The rest of the cubs laughed.

The gang didn't like being laughed at by second graders.

They quit the game.

"We'll see *you* later," said Too-Tall as they left.

Sister saw the whole thing. She wondered if Herbert was *trying* to make Too-Tall mad. It wasn't a very smart thing to do. But what could you expect from a goofy, goony guy?

Sister was sure of it a couple days later.

That's when they had the All-Grades Field Day. It had special rules. Cubs didn't have to compete in their own grades. Sister was a fast runner. She could run faster than many third and fourth graders. She signed up for the all-grades dash.

Brother signed up for the ball toss and the soccer kick.

The Too-Tall gang was there, but they didn't sign up for anything. They were there looking for trouble.

"Herbert," said Too-Tall, "how about racing me one on one? I'll give you a head start."

Too-Tall had a plan. First, he would step on Herbert's heels. Next, he would run over him. Then he would push him off the track.

"Happy to," said Herbert. "But I don't need a handicap."

Sister came in third in the all-grades dash.

Brother won the ball toss. He

came in second in the soccer kick.

And Herbert beat Too-Tall. *He beat him hopping on one foot!*

Too-Tall was very mad. His whole gang was very mad.

Brother decided to keep an eye on Herbert in case something happened. But nothing happened.

A few days later, Sister got off the school bus with big news.

"Guess what, Mama," she said. "We're going on a school trip. We're going to visit Farmer Ben's farm!"

"That *is* exciting," said Mama. "When will it be?"

"Tomorrow!" said Sister. "We have to take lunch."

"I think we can handle that," said Mama.

"I took that trip in second grade," said Brother.

"How was it?" asked Sister.

"It was cool," said Brother. "Farmer Ben's is a great place. He has these huge machines. He's got all kinds of animals—he even has a bull."

When Sister woke up the next morning, she was all excited. But she couldn't remember why.

Then she remembered.

Today was the day of the class trip.

"Here's your lunch box," said

Mama after Sister came downstairs.

"What's in it?" she asked.

"You'll see when you get there," said Mama.

Sister peeked.

Peanut butter and jelly sandwich and a thermos of milk.

Perfect, she thought.

Sister got off the school bus.

The trip bus was waiting.

Soon they were driving over a bumpy back road. Sister sat with Lizzy Bruin. They would stay together all day.

Teacher Jane sat at the front.

"Class," said Teacher Jane, "we

shall be at Ben's farm soon. Remember: A farm is a very exciting place. But it can be a dangerous place. Ben has some large animals. He has some big machines. So there will be no running around. There will be no walking off."

"We must be here," said Sister. "I see some cows."

"I see some pigs," said Lizzy.

The bus pulled to a stop. The class was very excited. Teacher Jane stood up.

"Please listen," she said. "When you get off the bus, form two lines. Girls in one line. Boys in the other. Both lines in size order."

The cubs formed two lines. The lines were side by side.

Lizzy was taller than Sister. She went to the back.

Not to be near Lizzy was bad enough. But now Sister was with Marcia, Gwen, and Jill.

"As we walk," said Teacher Jane, "we're going to hold hands. Reach out and take the hand of the cub next to you."

Oh no! thought Sister.

One guess who was next to Sister.

That's right.

Herbert Harold Armfoot III.

That was all Marcia, Gwen, and Jill needed.

"Look who's holding ha-ands! Look who's holding ha-ands!" they sang.

Sister was steamed. She gritted her teeth. She wanted to pop them. But she kept her cool.

"Stay together," said Teacher Jane. "Hold hands as we go from place to place. Farmer Ben, they're all yours."

"This way, cubs!" cried Farmer Ben. "First stop, the chicken yard!"

What a noise! What a mess! *What a smell!* A great cry of "Pee-yew!" went up from the class.

"The next cub that says 'pee-yew,'" said Teacher Jane, "will go back and wait on the bus. I apologize, Farmer Ben."

Farmer Ben just laughed.

"Cubs, would you like to feed the chickens?" he said.

"Yes!" shouted the cubs.

Mrs. Ben held out a big basket

of chicken feed. The cubs took the feed. They threw it over the fence and into the yard. The chickens clucked and pecked.

"Line up and hold hands," cried Teacher Jane over the noise of the chickens. "It's time to move on."

"Next stop, the dairy barn!" cried Farmer Ben.

There were twenty-six cows in the dairy barn. They were all hooked up to a big machine.

"What's that machine?" asked Sister.

"It's a milking machine," said Herbert.

They were still holding hands.

The dairy barn was so interesting they forgot to let go.

That got Marcia, Gwen, and Jill started again.

"Look who's holding ha-ands! Look who's holding ha-ands!" they sang.

Sister dropped Herbert's hand like it was a hot potato.

"Line up!" said Teacher Jane. "It's time to move on."

"Next stop, the machinery barn," said Farmer Ben.

The machinery barn was next to the dairy barn. Ben showed them many kinds of farm machines. They were as big as monsters.

It had been a long morning.

"Ready for lunch?" said Farmer Ben.

"YA-A-AY!" cheered the cubs.

"Line up and hold hands," said Teacher Jane. "It's time for lunch."

Lined up and holding hands, the class left the machine barn.

Outside they saw a real monster—a living, breathing, snorting monster.

It was Brutus. It was Farmer Ben's bull.

He snorted and pawed the ground. He lowered his head and shook his horns.

The cubs were very afraid.

But they had nothing to fear. Brutus was in a pen. It was a bull pen. It had a fence made out of big, heavy logs.

But the bull pen also had a gate . . . *and somebody had left it open!*

Brutus lowered his head and charged.

The cubs screamed.

They all broke and ran.

Except for Sister and Herbert. Herbert pulled on Sister's hand. But she wouldn't move. She was frozen in her tracks.

The great snorting bull was coming at her like an express train.

Herbert let go of Sister's hand.

But he didn't run away. He ran along the bull pen fence. He climbed into the bull pen. He began to dance and yell and wave his arms.

"YAYA-YA-YAYA!" he yelled.

He waved his arms like a very fast windmill.

His dancing shook the ground.

Brutus slowed down. He looked at Herbert out of the corner of his eye.

He stopped.

Then the express train turned around . . . and came after Herbert.

Herbert jumped out of the bull pen.

Brutus smashed into the log fence with a giant KLUNK!

All he got for his trouble was a big headache.

Farmer Ben closed the gate.

Teacher Jane helped Sister.

"Good job, young fellow," said Farmer Ben. "You did the right thing. How did you know what to do?"

"Well," said Herbert, "bulls happen to be one of my favorite things. I know they have good hearing and poor eyesight. So I knew I had to make some noise and wave my arms. As for the idea that red makes them mad—that's wrong. Bulls are almost color-blind."

There was lots more to see after lunch. They saw the pigs. They rode the horses. They petted the lambs.

Sister held Herbert's hand the rest of the day.

She needed something to hold on to.

"Then what happened?" asked Brother.

"The bull turned around and chased Herbert instead," said Sister.

"Wow!" said Brother. "I can see the headline: 'Goofy, Goony Guy Saves Girl!'"

"I'll have no more 'goofy, goony' talk," said Mama. "Now finish your breakfast. It's almost time for the school bus."

Sister took the seat Lizzy had

saved for her. She looked all around. Herbert wasn't on the bus.

That was okay with Sister.

She was glad that Herbert had known what to do at the farm. But she was still worried. Everyone had thought they were girlfriend and boyfriend before. What would they think now? Marcia, Gwen, and Jill would giggle their brains out.

"Herbert's not on the bus," said Sister.

"He's walking to school today," said Lizzy.

"Oh," said Sister. "How do you know?"

"I saw him," said Lizzy. "He lives

near me. He said he didn't like all the fuss."

"That makes two of us," said Sister.

Sister could tell it was going to be a long day.

She could tell as soon as she and Herbert took their seats.

It wasn't just Marcia, Gwen, and Jill. It was the whole class.

They kept looking.

They passed notes.

They whispered behind their hands.

Teacher Jane saw what was going on. She decided to put a stop to it.

"I'm sure," she said, "that we all had an interesting time yesterday. So we're going to work hard today. We will make up for lost time."

And did they *ever*!

They went to the board and did short division.

They did number work in their number workbooks.

They had spelling.

They read aloud.

That was all before lunch.

After lunch, Teacher Jane had a meeting. It was for the Tree Watchers' Club. They were called upon to tell about their trees.

Lizzy had four trees. They were

oak, pine, maple, and fir.

Sister had six. They were oak, pine, maple, fir, spruce, and elm.

Herbert had *seventeen*! He gave his whole list.

"That's very good, Herbert," said Teacher Jane. "Especially since you're new in class. Er, Herbert, what was the last tree?"

"Osage orange, ma'am," said Herbert.

"I beg your pardon," said Teacher Jane.

"Osage orange," said Herbert.

"Is there one here at school?" asked Teacher Jane.

"Yes, ma'am," said Herbert.

"Er, the others may not know that tree," said Teacher Jane. "Please tell us about it."

"It's a fine tree," said Herbert. "It has oval leaves. Its fruits are big, bumpy green balls. The fruits are bigger than baseballs. They give off sticky sap. The sap smells like oranges."

"Thank you, Herbert," said Teacher Jane. "You know a lot about trees."

Sister knew what Herbert was going to say.

"Yes, ma'am," said Herbert. "Trees are one of my favorite things."

After Tree Watchers' Club they had gym.

They pushed back the desks and chairs.

Then they did jumping jacks, squat thrusts, and toe touches until the bell rang.

The class headed for the door.

"Sister, William, Arnold . . . ," said Teacher Jane. "Please help put back the desks and chairs."

It took a few minutes to put the desks and chairs back.

Sister walked quickly to the bus. She didn't want to miss it.

The buses were still there.

They were filling up fast.

Her bus was about to leave.

If she hurried, she could make it.

But something caught her eye.

It was way off in the corner of the yard.

It was the Too-Tall gang and Herbert.

And they were pushing Herbert around!

They were near the tree Herbert had told about.

And they were knocking him down!

She looked around for help. But there wasn't anybody. Herbert really needed help.

Her bus was leaving. There was nobody to help except Sister. She thought about yesterday. She thought about the bull. She knew what she had to do.

"YOU LET HIM ALONE!" she screamed. *"LET HIM ALONE NOW!"*

She ran to help Herbert as fast as her legs could carry her.

They were doing that old bully's trick. One gang member would kneel down behind Herbert and another pushed him over.

"You stop that!" shouted Sister. "You leave him alone!"

"Or you'll do *what*?" said Too-Tall.

"Or I'll tell my brother!" shouted Sister.

"Hear that, gang?" said Too-Tall. "She's gonna tell her brother."

The gang laughed. They pushed Herbert over again.

"You stop that!" shouted Sister.

She tried to get past Too-Tall. But she couldn't: He was too big.

Then she saw something. Every time they knocked Herbert down, he got up closer to that crazy tree. Its fruits *were* bigger than baseballs.

It was almost as if Herbert had a plan.

Now they were *under* the tree.

The next time they knocked him

over, he did a flip. He climbed up into the tree. Herbert shook the branches.

Great sticky Osage oranges came raining down.

BONK, BONK, BONK went the big, hard fruits. They bounced off the gang's noggins.

"OUCH, YIPE, YUCK!" went the gang as they got out from under the tree.

The gang was so angry.

They didn't like being beaten by a second grader.

"We'll get you for this!" shouted Too-Tall.

"What's going on over there?"

called Teacher Jane. She was at the school steps. She was on the way to her car.

The gang left. They were still shaking their fists. But they left.

There were Osage oranges all over the ground. The whole place smelled like oranges.

"You could have been hurt," said Sister.

Herbert climbed down from the tree.

"Thank you very much for your help," he said.

"I don't understand boys sometimes," said Sister. "Why didn't you run away? They're much bigger than you. Next, you'll be telling me that you can take care of yourself, you're a black belt in karate, and karate is one of your favorite things! Well, if you ask me—"

"Brown," said Herbert.

"Brown what?" said Sister.

"Brown belt," said Herbert. "I never got to black belt."

"Oh," said Sister.

"You missed your bus," said Herbert.

"So did you," said Sister. "But that's okay. I've walked home before."

"Me too," said Herbert. "Maybe we can walk home together."

"Okay," said Sister.

So off they went, walking, skip-ping, and running.

They even held hands part of the way.

It was just like Mama said: You can't have too many friends.

Stan and Jan have been writing and illustrating books about the Berenstain Bears for many years. They live on a hillside in Bucks County, Pennsylvania, a place that looks a lot like Bear Country. They see deer, wild turkeys, rabbits, squirrels, and woodchucks through their studio window almost every day—but no bears. The Bears live inside their hearts and minds.

Stan and Jan have two sons. Their names are Michael and Leo. Leo is a writer. Michael is an illustrator. They help their parents write and illustrate the books. Stan and Jan have four grandchildren. One of them can already draw pretty good bears.